The last time I saw my friend the Bear he was adrift on the Thames River,
about to vanish under the arches of old London Bridge. I certainly didn't expect
to see him again. But chance encounters can have extraordinary outcomes.

I've always loved Shakespeare's *A Midsummer Night's Dream*. Ever since
I saw an old black-and-white movie of the play, I have been excited by the idea
of a magical forest populated with mischievous faeries. It was in that mysterious
place that I found inspiration and the chance to give the Bear a return performance.
And if you look closely you might even recognize some of the other players.

GREGORY ROGERS

GREGORY ROGERS

MIDSUMMER KNIGHT

A NEAL PORTER BOOK
ROARING BROOK PRESS
NEW MILFORD, CONNECTICUT

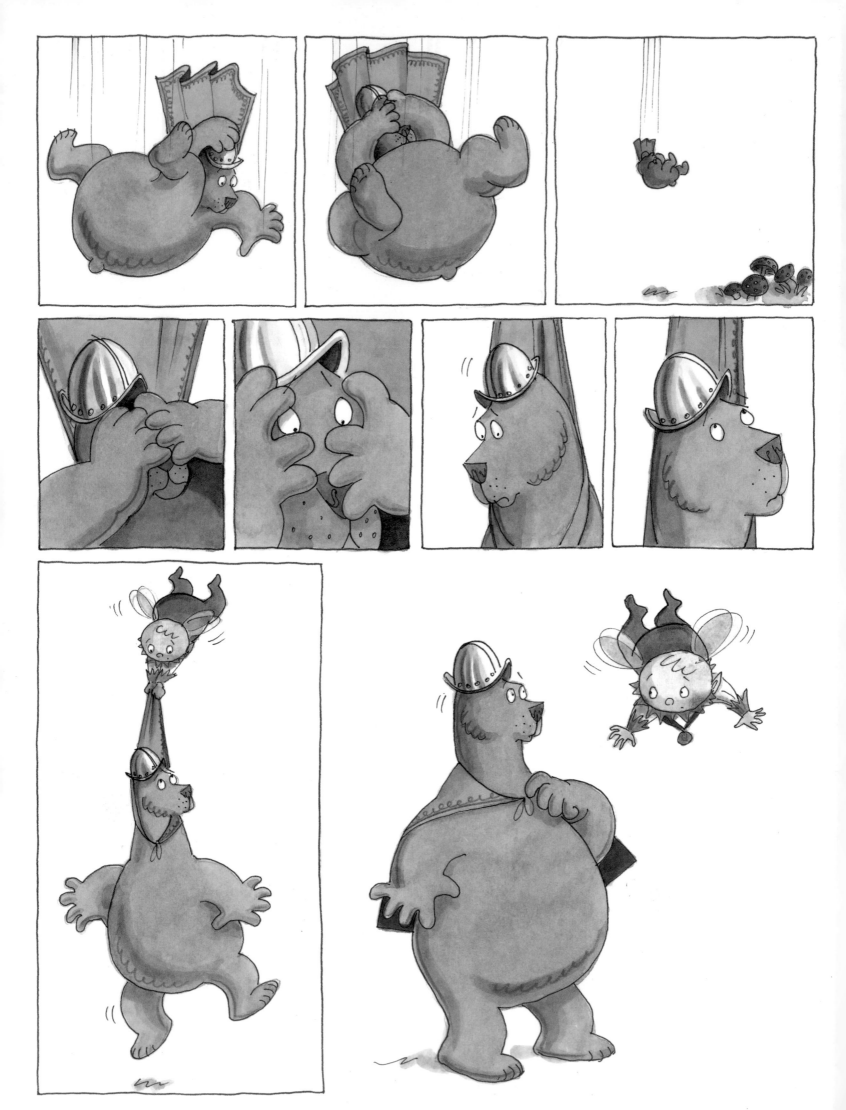

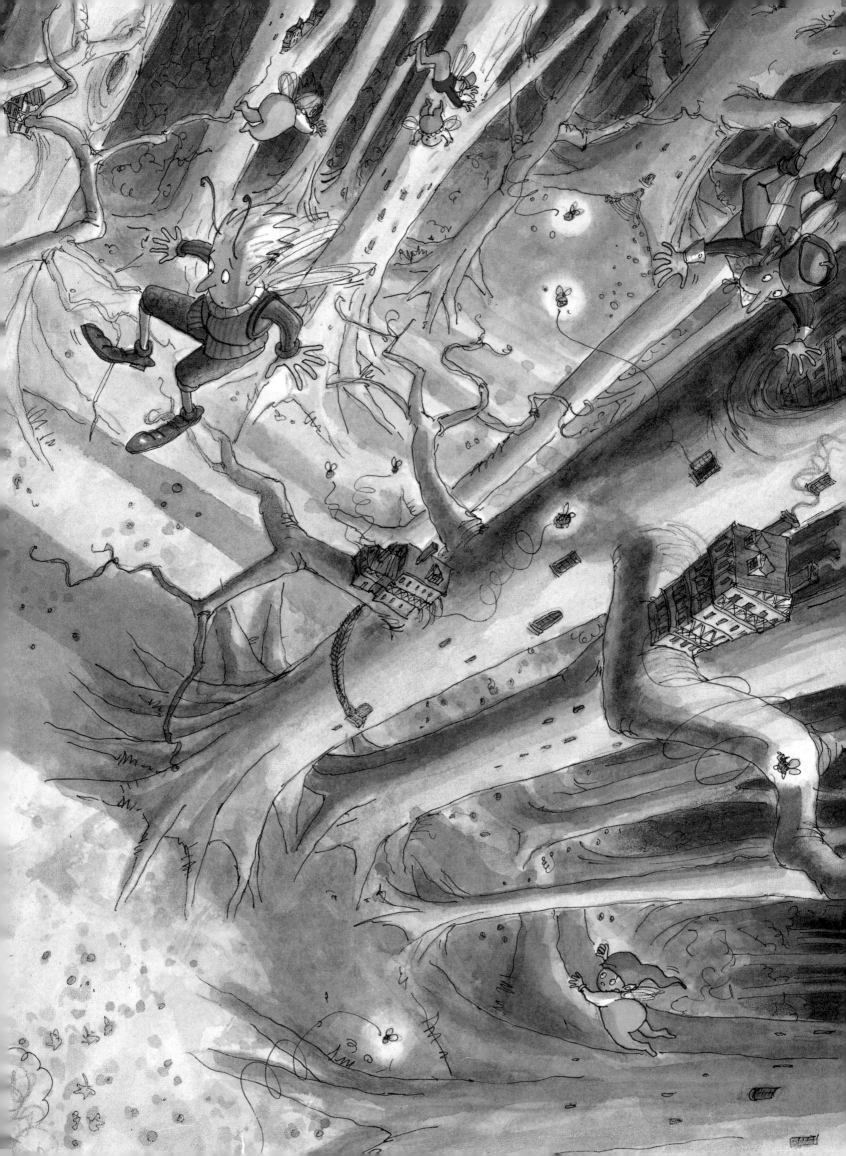

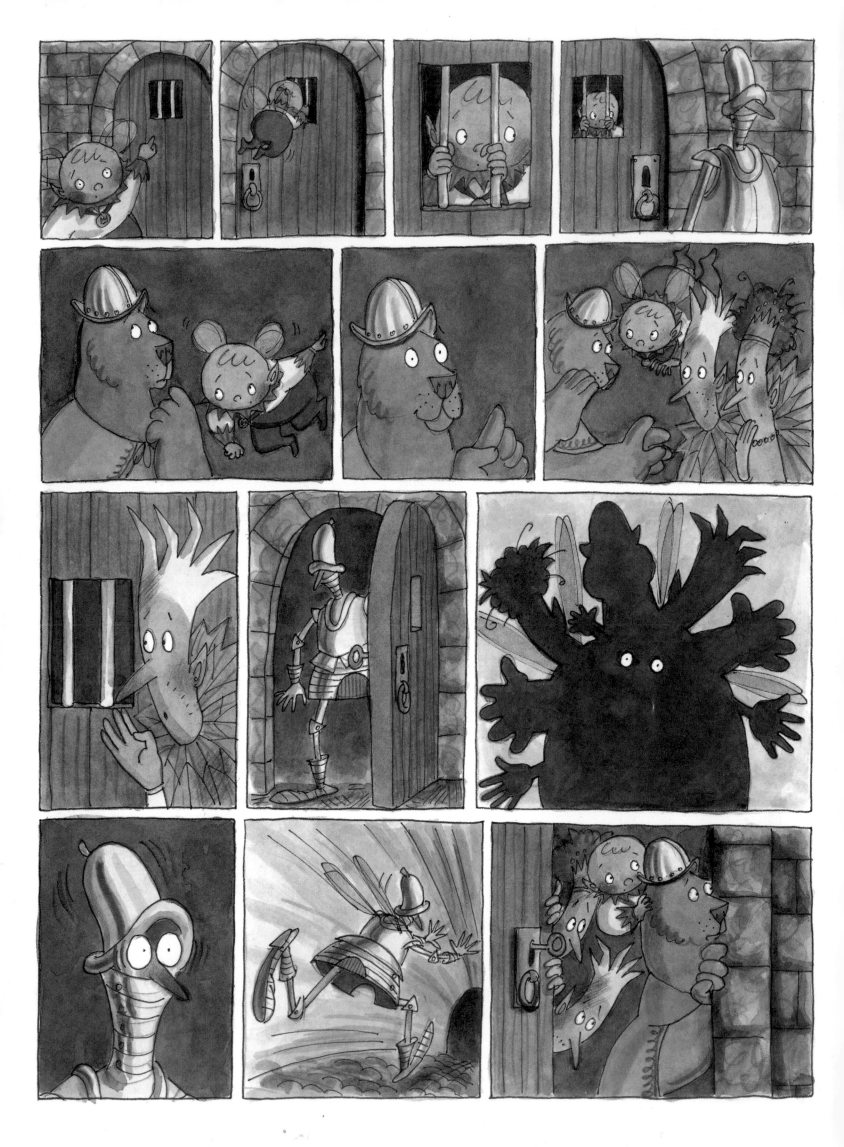

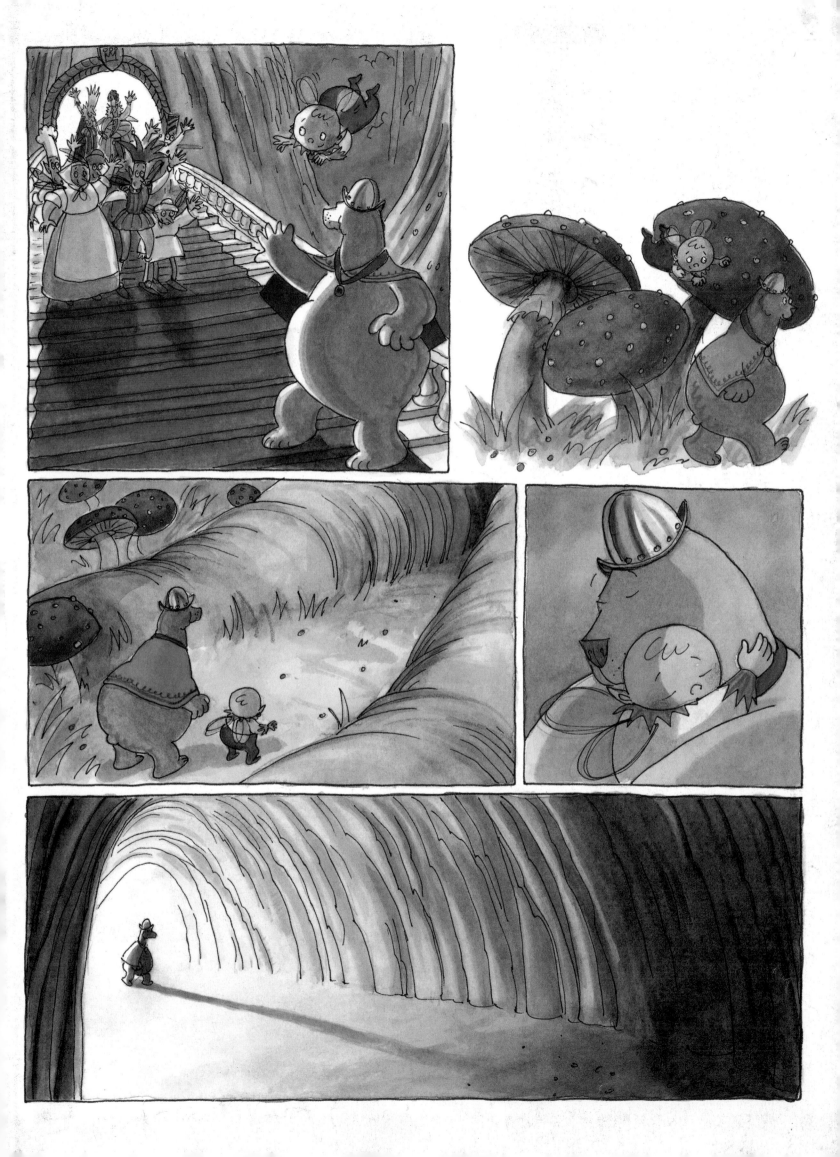

ACKNOWLEDGEMENTS

Thanks to Sienna Brown for sharing his journey with me, Erica Wagner and Jodie Webster who kept the wind in my sails, Margaret Connolly for keeping the waters calm along the way, Neal Porter who is the beacon on foreign shores and Bart, Harry and Pudding for keeping the home lights burning for when I arrived back at port. Thanks to the Australia Council for keeping the boat afloat.

Distributed in Canada by H. B. Fenn and Company Ltd.

Cataloging-in-Publication Data is on file at the Library of Congress
ISBN-13: 978-1-59643-183-6
ISBN-10: 1-59643-183-0

Roaring Brook Press books are available for special promotions and premiums.
For details contact: Director of Special Markets, Holtzbrinck Publishers

First American Edition May 2007
Book Design by Gregory Rogers
Printed in the United States of America

3   5   7   9   10   8   6   4   2